Unlocked Diary

Voice Of Heart

Published By

Unlocked Diary

Voice Of Heart

Penned By

Mary Majhi

ABOUT THE AUTHOR

Mary Majhi, born on 14 February 1995, from the Land of Art and Culture, Mayurbhanj, Odisha. Owner of Art and Craft business. From her childhood she is fond of writing and painting. She was awarded with many prizes and certificates. She was also a chess champion in district level. In future she wants to publish a novel.

ACKNOWLEDGEMENT

I wish to express my gratitude to Poetry World

Org. for a grant that made publishing my book

"UNLOCKED DIARY" possible.

Hearty thanks to my readers, who have stucked

with my poems.

Mary Majhi

Odisha

June, 2020

INDEX

LIFESPAN 13

TUBERROSE 14

POLITICS 15

CLOUDS 16

SEASHORE 17

SOLDIER 18

GARLAND 19

MIRROR 20

EVENTIDE IN SIKKIM 21

RAINBOW 22

SPRING 23

JUNE... 24

DREAMCATCHER 25

UNDERWATER... 26

ERROR 27

CUP OF TEA 33

MOTHER 34

WOMANHOOD 35

INDIAN SUMMER 36

PATHWAY 38

NATIVITY 40

POETRY WORLD ORG.

VOICE OF HEART 42

EMPTINESS IN THE DARK 43

GURUDONGMAR 45

MORNING 49

ARTIST LIFE IN CORONAVIRUS PANDEMIC 50

THE UNUSUAL TIMES 51

<u>LIFESPAN</u>

The cycle of lifespan,

From origination to conclusion

The wheel of life revolves,

Like planets in the solar system.

From the first cry of infant,

To the death's sorrowful lament.

At the end karmas sum up,

And thus one gets rebirth.

Nothing is fixed or permanent,

Try to walk in the path of enlightment.

Nature of everything is illusory and ephemeral.

They come into being and dissolve after all.

Life embodies this flux in the aging process.

With due time everything decays.

<u>TUBERROSE</u>

Milky, white and aromatic,

Blossomed in the rays of moonlight.

In that pure dusky midnight,

Her aroma spread far and wide.

Was it a fantasy or magical time?

She was shining more radiant in the moonbeam.

They loved and accompanied each other very deep.

As the dawn arrived, moon disappeared leaving her
lonely.

<u>POLITICS</u>

In the world of unreality and illusion,

It's well to stay in seclusion.

People live with masked faces,

Made of poisonous bloody flesh.

They rule all over illegally,

With the power of dirty money.

Constructed the Kingdom of violence and sin.

That can be attocities or corruption indeed.

Kept the law in an enclosed fist,

Politics plays here like a gamble bet.

This is the World of fake and phoney.

Not less than any puppet display.

<u>CLOUDS</u>

Fluffy cotton balls in the sky,

Looked up above so high.

Sometimes seemed as white fairies,

Other times appeared like birds plumage.

For me the sky was Jumbotron,

In the darkness of leaden.

Stars and moon shed their enlights,

During day sun rules over the reddish golden clouds.

Floating, hanging like Narcissus,

Natural, bleached blooms all over the sky.

<u>SEASHORE</u>

Gleamy eyes observed the tides,

Relaxed my soul, the sound of the waves.

Hair curls kissed my briny chin,

Rushing wind forced it to spin.

The Empyrean and marine smooching.

Amorously I was watching.

Sea was wrapped with blue satin,

Waves were decorated with white jewels and shells.

Wildly danced each and every time.

Messing around the design of the coastline.

Repeated the dance each time,

Lost myself in her amusement every time.

<u>SOLDIER</u>

Keeping the heart filled with adore,

In every drop of blood packed with force.

Warriors made of this soil,

Enemies lose ground and repel.

They sacrifice their life with brave heart,

To save the Nation they become mortal.

Deep inside the skin bullet penetrates,

Still they fight to defeat the foes.

Delightly they become martyr,

The Nation salutes them with deep respect and honor.

They are the real heroes of the Motherland,

Fought with power till the end.

<u>GARLAND</u>

Waked up on a Monday morn,

Chirping birds and dazzling sun made more adorn.

My ears were blessed hearing the ringing bell,

That was echoing loud from the temple.

Plucked the flowers with excitement,

Thought of weaving beautiful garland.

Filled the needle with thread of inches,

Pushed petals and rolled bilva leaves with choice.

Tatted the flowers in the string,

Snowy, ruby, bisque formed the ring.

His beauty was mesmerizing,

When Lord Shiva was garlanded with adoring.

<u>MIRROR</u>

Piece of silver glass,

Glazing, shining resolute.

Holding the candour with embrace,

Can I call it a truth speaker?

Since childhood till now,

She made me remember myself better.

Lapse of time and thus I've grown,

Sometimes I see myself successful and brave,

At times coward and broken.

The place where I stare my body shape,

My long hairs and physiognomy very often.

Companion of every stage of life,

Who saw my tears and smiles.

Helped me to speak with mine,

Stepping to the growing age, she always notifies me.

<u>EVENTIDE IN SIKKIM</u>

The dusk was alluring,

Coldness made me trembling.

Unutterable inexpressible beauty,

Filled joy the land of visionary.

Midnight frozen raining,

Bonfire made it more pleasanting.

We enjoyed all get-together,

It will be recalled forever.

The ambience was filled with tranquility,

Our vocalize disrupted the quietude.

It was the dreamy magical night,

My eyes observed every sight.

Not less than any fairy land.

Watched the frosty mountains from casement,

Peaks were gleaming with illumination of moon.

Captured my eyes from the room.

<u>RAINBOW</u>

The rain drops started kissing the Earth floor,

Wet clothes in the rope danced hither and thither.

My window glasses turned blur,

Prayed Almighty to show the vibgyor.

Darted towards the terrace,

Mounted gasping for breath.

Up above clouds were moving with grace,

No sooner my eyes caught the beautiful spot.

Reflection, refraction, dispersion of light

Scientifically meteorological phenomenon

Arc formed by illuminated droplets,

Appeared in the sky resulting in a spectrum.

Bow of good luck, smile and hope

Almighty showers his blessings,

Floating clouds were draped

With bright VIBGYOR paint.

<u>SPRING</u>

Smelled aromatic fresh air,

Eyes watched lovely floral nature.

Chirping birds and the beautiful atmosphere,

This is how spring gives its signature.

Fruitful of productive season,

Birds busy in building nests.

Thanks Almighty for the creation,

The month seemed full of zest.

Butterflies moved all over,

Spreading their vibrant wings.

Flying to and fro.

With the Nature's melodious song.

Bring spring to the life too, melodious and sunshine.

Sow the seeds now, for enjoying ripening results in time.

<u>JUNE</u>

Month of welcoming monsoons,

Sometimes I watch floating clouds.

At intervals rays of sunbeams,

Dry lands swamping with floods.

Overgrown verdant meadows,

Glowing bulbs or droplets of water.

Charming drenched blossom flowers,

Farmers give gratitude to the creator.

My heart leaps a bit.

Partly sunny and rainfall,

My eye catches a lovely sight

That's the rainbow made my day cheerful.

<u>DREAMCATCHER</u>

Beautifully swinging to and fro,

Decorated with feathers and beads.

Sign of good luck and life grow,

Represents positive energy and good dreams.

Small hoop containing mesh horsehair,

Constructed with string or yarn.

Known as dreamcatcher,

Protect people from nightmares.

Acts like a spider web,

Bad dreams gets trap.

Everyone wants fortune to grab,

Neutralize bad energy, whether you're

Asleep or awake.

<u>UNDERWATER</u>

The world of peace,

Quiet, calm and deep.

The place of aquatics,

Dived inside the water with creep.

A series of blue waves, making spherical shapes.

My heart leaped a bit,

Merrily sang melodious harmony within it.

Different from our fake world,

Real and peaceful all around,

The world of marine flora and fauna,

Attractive coral reefs and shells,

Hidden pearls and expensive gemstones.

<u>ERROR</u>

Every path I have trodden,

Before me was sudden.

But I travelled in them,

In the mid they became my dream.

Enjoyed them a lot,

Thinking that future dream was caught.

Thought myself great,

With lots of plan that was stored in the cart.

As I travelled through,

Found the path rough.

Felt little bitter,

Found good person very rare.

One day I saw darkness,

Everyone was packed with selfishness.

Felt suffocated in the end,

But nothing left behind.

Except my empty hand,

I trodden the wrong path.

Realized every fault,

But it was the end of the life.

My soul left my body stabbed with knife.

<u>RHODODENDRON</u>

POETRY WORLD ORG.

The dawn was slightly murky,

Travelled through the land of Yamthung valley.

Roads surrounded by mountain glaciers,

Spotted hot springs everywhere.

My feet stepped into the valley of flowers,

Amazingly watched the beauty with peace.

Dark red velvet bunched flora,

Blossomed all over covering the area.

Their beauty attracted more towards them,

I lost myself in the wild floral garden.

Kissed them, touched them, plucked one

Tucked it in the hairs of mine,

"RHODO" the rose of Sikkim,

The trees are "DENDRON"

Registered as the National flower of Nepal.

Presented Heaven on Earth after all,

Dreamt of building a home.

Surrounded by flowers and waterfall.

Enjoyed each and every moment there,

With passage of time, packed my memories with care.

<u>CUP OF TEA</u>

Love of every morning,

Accompanied with newspaper reading.

A cup full of warm tea,

Miss my sticky lips to sip it.

Choice of every season,

Relaxes more in winter and monsoon.

<u>MOTHER</u>

Her love is priceless,

Gives blessings for success.

The queen of home,

Who hides her pain but gives smiley welcome.

Her care is heart melting,

Graciously handles everything.

Her lap gives peaceful sleep,

Her hug gives warmth in deep.

For me she is my guardian angel,

Not less than any lucky gem.

Works everyday without salary,

In need becomes nurse professionally.

The God who brought me into this world,

For me thanking her and expressing her is very hard.

<u>WOMANHOOD</u>

35

Supreme being sublime creation,

Human origin from ovaries preparation,

Menstrual gifted to womanhood,

Became her dignity and should be proud.

She is superior let's praise her,

Plays vital role in every part of life,

Unable to describe them all in brief,

Make her proud with respect and love.

<u>INDIAN SUMMER</u>

The period of warm season,

Occurring in late autumn.

Thought with deep emotion,

Asked myself "When will I get this period of
happiness?"

Working hard to achieve success

Already crossed life's early stage.

The period of killing frost,

Presenting good times with autumn mist.

Spreading tentacles from sunrise to set.

Countryside becoming more flamboyant.

Lost myself in dreamy eyes,

Asked myself "When will I get this re-beautifying
sight?"

As the Nature longing for beautiful sunshine

My soul dreams for prosperity every time.

Deep core inside cried with exhaustion

Still finding hope for good fortune.

<u>PATHWAY</u>

A twist came in my life,

With a beautiful sunrise.

Met someone who gave me smile,

Accepted it with great divine.

Became addicted to someone,

Like red chilled wine.

Drived myself all crazy,

Despite of being busy, felt cozy.

Found pleasure in walking with him,

Became rich by getting a lucky gem.

Garden filled with flowers,

And his surrounding packed with wild aromas.

One day I found the moon with smiling cold mask,

When we were walking beside the busy road in dusk.

Our hands were locked tightly,

A slow wind was crossing us perfectly,
for binding us in a relation

Every evening was waiting with preparation,

After some time eyes seemed gloomy,

Lips became sticky,

Wanted to share lot things,

Time came for separating,

Seemed all things wrong.

Our heart stopped for a moment,

A bridge diverted our way of enjoyment.

Felt my locked fingers free,

Occupied fingers left the place,

Vacant places was then filled with jealousy air,

Found the loneliness so near.

<u>NATIVITY</u>

Finding out the meaning of life,

With a little hope,

Became difficult for me to write an epilogue

Thinking day and night,

With this puzzled brain fight.

No way seems in my sight,

Where I can get a scope of light.

Became clown in this world of unknown,

Everyone laughed at me wearing devils horn.

The fear of emptiness grown,

Remembered the day when I was born.

The day of love celebrated everywhere,

Full of red roses and kisses like sapphire.

I lost myself in the world of love and divine,

The day I took birth was valentine.

Someone whispered in my ear,

Still you are alone my dear.

Getting a true partner,

Is only in the life of lucky lovers.

<u>VOICE OF HEART</u>

Don't drain out tear drops,

Still I am having a little hope.

In this busy inhumane world,

No one hears my painful words.

Half of my life has already gone,

Still I am feeling alone,

I want to share my feeling with seashore,

If he could reach to my deep heart core.

I too want to know his feelings,

Who has hidden so many things

When I sit near him,

He comes near, kisses feet of mine

Within a blink of second,

He leaves me alone and moves backward.

With a lot of pain my heart cries,

Still I go near him as a new sunrise.

EMPTINESS IN THE DARK

43

Emptiness kissing my body,

Under the moonlight sky.

Encircled with silence,

Buzz of insects breaking that calmness.

Breeze whispering melodious tune,

Unsympathetic hitting my skin.

Darkness of night embracing me,

Found peace between struggles of mine.

POETRY WORLD ORG.
POETRY WORLD ORG.

<u>GURUDONGMAR</u>

POETRY WORLD ORG.

The first view of the sacred lake,

Was like something I haven't felt.

My heart skipped a bit or two,

Found myself in the highest altitude.

After facing a lot of hardship,

Reached there with masterstroke.

The environment was soothing to the mind,

A blessed calmness in the entire area prevailed,

The snow fed milky water of the lake,

Land of blue sheep and the yaks.

The beauty was breath taking,

Pristine white water gushing.

Lush whitish green valleys and countless waterfalls,

Snowy mountains, curvy roads, valley of floral.

The blessed water of the lake Gurudongmar,

Believed to possess the miraculous power.

Gaspingly prayed with the stacked stones,

My eyes caught something precious,

Merrily felt more blessed,

Watched the clouds that formed Trident.

MORNING

Reddish golden clouds,

Floating all over making crowds.

With deep penetrating rays,

Making the dawn go forever.

Rays of hope,

Rays of love,

Knocking my window pane so brightly,

Blowing darkness away.

Almighty showers his blessings in such a way.

Eradicates all the obstacles.

ARTIST LIFE IN CORONAVIRUS PANDEMIC

Present situation of pandemic,

Made artist life effective.

Spending time in lockdown throes,

Deep inside them created woes.

Everybody accepted the stage of isolation,

Created artworks with deep sublimation.

Artist's dependant on their art for survival,

Faced acute hardships of economic fall.

Spreading awareness through online exhibition,

Highlighting posters of captions and precautions.

Painting exhibitions have been cancelled or postponed,

Art buyers are now out of the spot.

Social media became the only medium,

Through which, artists can show their creativity overall.

<u>THE UNUSUAL TIMES</u>

Name that created fear,

Assassinate the world superior.

Spread its tentacles,

Creating restlessness,

In the form of virus,

Spreading awareness,

Travelled everywhere,

Desisting get-together.

Knowledge of sanitation,

Eradicating corona is mission.

Became the breaking news,

Moratorium to become huge.

World covered with taciturnity,

Busiest roads turned empty.

Masks became instant weapon,

Honestly fighting back is the great action.

POETRY WORLD ORG.